THE BACHELOR KNIGHT

Deborah Simmons

CHAPTER ONE

"My lord! My lord!"

Heedless of the shout, Sir Berenger Brewere stood staring into the distant hills. Although the peaks were too far away and hardly steep, they rose taller than the surrounding lands. And yet he surveyed those nearby with a mixture of pride and longing. There were no mountains here, no rocky crags, only gently rolling slopes. *But all of it is mine.*

"Sir Brewere!" The use of his surname roused Beren at last, and he turned slowly to cover his lapse. How many years would it take him to recognize his own title? King Edward had bestowed upon him the barony and fiefdom for services rendered during the war in Wales, and Beren lived like a lord. Why could he not answer as one?

Beren sighed, moving away from the heights to the young squire who shouted to him so eagerly. What had sent the boy racing to find him? A call to arms? A visit from the king? Farman, a youth Beren had plucked from obscurity, was too easily excited. Whatever it was, Beren suspected he would have to put aside his half-formed plans to view the distant hills more closely and attend to some business of knighthood, whether it be war or justice that commanded his attention.

Farman halted before him, a bit breathless after his run from the castle to the grassy bank where Beren waited. "'Tis a messenger, my lord, bidding you away!"

'Twas from the king then, Beren thought. In years past, he had served other lords, but now he was vassal to none except Edward himself.

"A summons to court?" Beren asked. He was not certain where the king was in residence, but he knew the place would likely be overrun by fools and greedy, jealous courtiers—a situation he little liked. But Beren hid his distaste from his squire as he began to stride back toward the castle that bespoke his allegiance, if not to the court, to Edward himself.

"No!" Farman said. "'Tis a summons, aright, but not from the king. 'Tis a demand that you go at once to a place called Brandeth, at the behest of someone called St. Leger."

For a moment, all around Beren faded away at the mention of his old patron, Clement St. Leger. He drew in a harsh breath. *Brandeth.* 'Twas a name he had not considered in years, though he had begun his life there.

"The messenger was a bold fellow," Farman said in an outraged tone. "Lest you refuse, he would remind you of your oath. 'Recall to him his vow,'" Farman recited. "And then he left, without even waiting upon you, my lord!"

Stirred from his thoughts by Farman's indignation, Beren glanced down to see the youth was practically in a froth that anyone, let alone a mere messenger, should fail to make the proper obeisance to Sir Berenger Brewere, knight of the realm, holder of vast lands, baron to the king. Beren smiled, for he did not take himself quite as seriously as his squire.

Farman eyed him quizzically. "'Tis a jest, then, my lord?"

Beren's smile faded. "Nay, 'tis no jest, but a duty I am bound to fulfill." As if pausing his pace might mire him once more in memory, Beren walked swiftly now, the squire hurrying to keep up with him.

"But who is this St. Leger? Some foreign king? I have heard naught of him," Farman said.

"That does not make him less," Beren said, a bit sharply. The squire was becoming too full of himself, too accustomed to visits of the mighty and royal, to recall that a man was measured neither by fame nor bloodlines.

"But why should *you*, the greatest knight in the land, have to wait upon him?" Farman asked, stubbornly insistent upon his master's importance.

Beren halted, his gaze drawn to the distant peaks and beyond to that which he could not see: tall cliffs and crashing surf and a castle set amongst them. He murmured an answer, half to his squire and half to himself. "Because I swore an oath, and a knight's vow is broken only by death."

Ever alert, Beren had noted the changes in the lands around him, the seabirds on the wing and the tang in the air that spoke of the ocean. Old feelings stirred, unwelcome, making him irresolute for the first time in many a year, and he faltered for a moment before urging his destrier on.

He could not ignore the summons, though he had been tempted to send a messenger ahead to inquire about it. After all, he had many demands upon his time, including those of his own demesne, his obligations to the king and the courts of justice, and the people within his domain. Yet now he must leave all to be off on an errand the purpose of which he knew not.

Beren disliked approaching any situation without sufficient information, and he had not become successful by being unprepared. So he neared the holding with the wariness of a battle-hardened soldier, suspecting that things at Brandeth must be dire for Clement to send for him after all this time. But he saw no sign of siege or trouble of any kind, only the stark beauty of the cliffs.

Here, at last, were heights, rising from rocky stretches of beach into the very clouds, and Beren felt his heart pounding in an old, nearly forgotten rhythm. His first thought was that he had stayed away too long, his second that he never should have returned. Tearing his gaze away from the tall faces of stone, he looked to the road ahead, avoiding the twin distractions of emotion and memory, until he turned round the last outcropping and saw Brandeth.

Beren sucked in a harsh breath at the sight. He remembered it rising out of the rock face as if carved from the very elements, a vast and impenetrable defense. Yet now the castle appeared dwarfed by its surroundings, so much so that for a moment Beren wondered whether some part had been lost to war or fire.

But further scrutiny made him realize the place was the same, while *he* had changed. The keep that once had loomed so large within his vision had been dwarfed by the higher towers and sprawling walls of his own demesne, as well as others he had seen in endless travels.

Brandeth now appeared small and isolated, little more than an old-fashioned square keep with outbuildings surrounding it in a haphazard fashion. Quelling whatever feelings that threatened to erupt at that discovery, Beren studied it carefully, intent not upon reminiscence, but appraisal. Still, nothing appeared amiss, and lifting a hand, he sent his train forward along the path to the village.

Spilling out from the foot of Brandeth, the hamlet looked peaceful and prosperous, though tiny to Beren's jaded eyes. They passed through it quickly, climbing the rough track meant to keep invaders away, and at the castle gate, they halted. There Beren again surveyed the area carefully before continuing into the bailey, though there were enough men-at-arms to defend themselves against attack.

Clement had not come out to meet them, which could be a sign that he would not defer to his old squire. Beren frowned at the slight before thinking the man might be ill. That would explain his absence, but what of the summons itself? Why send for Beren after all these years? His mouth tightened, for he could provide no answers.

Outside the keep, Beren was relieved to be greeted in a quiet manner by a young man he did not know. But he could tell that Farman, ignorant of his master's history here, was disappointed by the lack of ceremony and cheers. Only Beren knew how unlikely the people of Brandeth were to welcome him in such a fashion. And even should they be so inclined, this was not a rich holding that could afford tournaments and such, a realization that somehow pained him.

Beren did not share his squire's exalted opinion of himself and did not mourn the absence of any pageantry proclaiming his arrival, for he knew his own failings. He had not wanted to come here and was glad that no one had appeared who knew what he was. Pride, one of a knight's sins, was plaguing him, and no doubt, he would be tested more before this visit was over.

Hardening his resolve, Beren took a handful of men and strode inside the hall, prepared to face his first demon. He stood tall, his gaze sweeping the room that immediately fell into silence. Although smaller than he recalled, the space was cleaner than his own hall. Little furniture was scattered about, but the walls were painted and covered with colorful tapestries that drew the eye.

Lest he pause too long in reluctant admiration, Beren dragged his attention away, letting it roam over the few people who stood by until it rested upon Hubard, the old bailiff. Wrinkled and stooped, the white-haired retainer posed no danger to anyone. Why, then, did Beren feel sorely set upon as the man moved toward him? He stiffened, his hand settling upon the hilt of his sword, but Hubard only bowed low, as befitting Beren's new stature. Then, to Beren's amazement, the old man began to weep.

Startled, Beren stepped forward, uncertain how to react until the bailiff lifted shining eyes to him once more. "Look at you! Just look at you, the greatest knight in all the land," Hubard said, shaking his head, while servants and residents crowded close, whispering. "Clement would be so proud."

Would be? Beren barely had a chance to note the man's choice of words when silence fell upon the hall once more. He glanced up to see a woman approach. She was slender and blond and as fair as the palest rose, the finest jewel, the clouds that rimmed the highest peaks. It was only after his heart began a fierce thundering in his chest that Beren recognized her as Guenivere, Clement's daughter.

"Welcome, Sir Brewere," she said, the title stiff and formal on her lips. "Thank you for coming."

The past that Beren sought to avoid rose up to meet him, and he lashed out at this unexpected vision of his former patron's daughter, little changed and yet wholly different. "Where is Clement?" he demanded.

"My father is dead," Guenivere said, and a spasm of pain marred her lovely face, only to be quickly masked. When had she learned to dissemble? When had she begun to hold herself so distant? Like a bright star, she was beautiful and yet untouchable. But then, hadn't she always been far out of his reach? The thought burned within him, as did her next words.

"'Twas I who summoned you," she said.

"You? Why?" Beren asked, angry that he had been dragged across the country for what? A woman's whim? His own torment?

Guenivere eyed him somberly as though waiting for Beren to reign in his temper. Although he told himself that she knew him not, her pale blue eyes seemed to hold the wisdom of the ages and insight into all things, including himself. Beren told himself it was a trick of the light, but her gaze held his, steady, unyielding, and he felt the flow of her strength, tender in its woman's guise, yet hard as steel.

"You once vowed to serve this family always and above all others," she said. "Do you not remember?"

Beren's jaw tightened. Of course, he remembered. His oath had brought him to this pass, though it was little to his liking.

"Now has come the time of my need. Will you refuse me?" Guenivere asked, her luminous eyes clear and questioning.

Beren stared at her dumbly, shying away from the expectation there, the accusation implicit in the blue depths. But there was nowhere to go. He could give no answer except one. Drawing a deep breath, he dropped upon one knee at her feet and bowed his head. "What is it you require of me, lady?" he asked, his voice suddenly hoarse, his throat thick.

The hall seemed even more silent that before, as if all those about them strained to hear or held their breath in anticipation. Beren felt as though the moment dragged on endlessly while he knelt before her, the past closing in on him, whether he willed it or no. It constricted his chest, choking the very air from his lungs. Then he heard her voice, soft and deliberate.

"I would ask you to marry me."

Beren's head jerked upward, followed quickly by his body as he shot to his feet in shocked confusion. Had he heard aright, or was his mind playing tricks on him? He stared at her, his breath coming harshly, his heart thundering. "Why?"

Unmoved by his obvious agitation, Guenivere answered him calmly, as if they were discussing the weather, not this incredible proposition. "Because my father is dead," she said. "I need a husband, else the lands that I own will be forfeit. My neighbors are clamoring to add Brandeth to their holdings, but I would choose none of them.

"Are you a widow then?" Beren asked, his thoughts a mad jumble.

"I have never married. Why would you think so?" Guenivere asked, a sharp edge to her voice for the first time since she had appeared before him, cool and remote.

Beren felt like a blabbering fool, rather than a warrior and a knight of some standing. "I had heard that you were betrothed some years ago and assumed..." Aware that he sounded like an idiot, Beren did not finish the sentence. Instead, he cleared his throat, lest his next words come out a desperate croak. "Why me?"

Guenivere glanced away. Was she unable to meet his gaze? Beren hesitated to speculate. "You are so strong and powerful that none will dispute your claim. And because you own far greater properties, you will not concern yourself with one tiny demesne." She turned to look at him directly once more. "I can maintain my heritage and protect my people, as I have these past few years during my father's illness."

Beren wasn't sure just what he had expected as an answer, but it wasn't this cold calculation. The past yawned before him now like an abyss, and he stepped back to take a deep, sustaining breath. He could not afford to be distracted. This was too important. Pushing back against the memories that threatened, he concentrated on the here and now, no matter how strange it might seem.

The king had long accused him of playing the bachelor knight when he had more than enough money and lands to take a wife. And lately Beren had considered the prospect of allying himself with one of the other large landowners through marriage. A union with a tiny, inconsequential barony such as this one was not what Edward had in mind, Beren was certain. And yet, how could he refuse?

His knight's oath bound him to protect and defend all women in distress, but he was bound here by more than that. On one bleak morning long ago when Clement had girded him as a knight, he had added a vow of his own. In heartfelt gratitude, Beren had pledged his sword to the St. Legers for all time. He had sworn to die for them, gladly. Now how could he refuse to do any less?

"Very well, Guenivere," Beren said, acutely aware of the sound of her name upon his lips, spoken aloud for the first time in his life. "I will marry you."

Either Guenivere was very sure of herself or very sure of him, for Beren soon found that all was in readiness for their nuptials. A priest appeared at once to perform the ceremony, so as to avoid any questions of validity. And Beren wondered if the haste was to prevent him from changing his mind. More likely, Guenivere didn't want to be able to change her mind, he thought ruefully.

In truth, Beren was glad of the speed, for he did not care to think too much upon what was happening. He was tired after the days of travel, weary in both body and spirit to find himself back at his journey's beginning, and unwilling to examine too closely the sudden and bizarre turn of events.

Beren told himself that he had no choice except to marry Guenivere, that his oath was what bound him, and that it was the only reason he had agreed to the union. But at the edges of his mind the past loomed, mocking his feeble attempts to explain away his actions.

The wedding itself took on an unreal aspect, and Beren went through the motions like one in a dream. It was only when he took Guenivere's hand in his that he was jolted to full awareness, for the touch of her fingers, soft yet firm, sent a rush of heat through him, startling in its intensity. Long-buried feelings flooded him, and he didn't know whether to shudder from the strength of them or bellow his denial.

Because he could do naught else, Beren added this new promise of marriage to his previous vow. Yet when he spoke, it was with a conviction born of more than duty, his chest suddenly tight with some unnamed emotion.

Bidden to kiss his bride, Beren hesitated, stunned at the very thought. When he did not move, Guenivere leaned up and brushed his cheek in a bloodless action that chilled him. Then it was over, and the feasting began.

As Guenivere called for the celebration, Beren stared numbly after her. He felt as though he had fought in one too many tournaments, smote so long and hard with sword and lance that his head rang from it. Drawing a harsh breath, he tried to recover himself, ruthlessly pushing aside all thoughts of other, earlier times in this hall.

Yet how could he? Among the figures of his own men, eager for the coming food and drink, Beren saw some familiar faces. Most appeared content, happy even, but did not some eye him with disapproval? If so, how could he blame them?

Restless, Beren stalked past the revelers as ale and wine began flowing freely, but there was nowhere else to go in the space. He paused near the tall doors, now thrown open wide in welcome, and halted there, staring out into the setting sun. But even that sight tugged at his memory, and he swore soft and low.

Although he considered going outside, the thought of old haunts stayed him, and Beren turned his head away. Noticing a movement out of the corner of his eye, he swung round to see a servant boy carrying too much wood upon his back. Anger surged inside of him, as well as something else, deeper and more stirring. "Who bade you bend yourself under such a weight?" Beren demanded.

"No one, my lord," the boy said, eyes wide with fear.

"Tell me, for I am your lord now," Beren said, though the words seemed to stick in his throat.

"N-no one, I swear! I was just trying to save myself another trip," the boy said. His innocent reply flustered Beren. With a grunt, he sent the boy on, only to find another servant eying him, obviously curious about his odd behavior. Beren drew a deep breath. He had reacted overmuch in this instance, but he knew all too well the backbreaking toil of one of lowly birth.

With that thought, the past crowded in on him again, and since he could go nowhere to escape it, he searched for a distraction. He found it in the sight of Guenivere, shining in the throng, and he looked upon her long, blond tresses with a kind of awe.

Warmth, unbidden and long denied, flooded him, driving away all the years of harsh conditions and battle, almost as if they had never been. Dangerous thoughts, Beren acknowledged, with a frown. Some knights were enamored of tender emotions, and some even wrote poetry, but not working knights, not a man who had to make his own way in the world.

Beren held back the tide of memory that threatened to engulf him, watching her now with new eyes, more calculating and less dewy with youth. And what he saw was a woman full-grown, past her girlhood, but possessing a rare beauty that was only enhanced by time. Why had she not married? What had Clement been thinking to leave his heritage in such disarray? Beren frowned once more. Guenivere said he had been ill. Perhaps he had not been thinking clearly.

Beren found it hard to think clearly himself as he watched her. She moved with an easy grace, as regal as her namesake, but with an open demeanor that encouraged small gifts from the children in the hall. Beren saw her bend down to receive a flower and give a kiss of thanks, and it seemed as though the path he had climbed for so long was shifting, altering the life he had led in some irrevocable fashion. He felt light-headed, as though he was falling, dropping from dizzying heights. Or had he merely returned to the ground where he belonged?

Shaking his head, Beren held himself tall and straight and apart, surveying all about him in the long habit of a warrior warily assessing his surroundings. And as the evening wore on,

Beren decided that he had good cause to be cautious.

He studied his bride with growing concern, for although she seemed to treat castle residents and servants and villeins with the same cordiality, she did not extend the same consideration to one of her guests, namely her husband. Even his own men were greeted warmly, while she stayed far from Beren.

He wondered whether his position on the edges of the gathering was the cause of her distance. So he moved among the revelers, inching closer to Guenivere, only to see her slip away. Her behavior might not be apparent to the casual observer, but Beren could hardly ignore it. And his temper, barely leashed since his arrival here, began to tug at its restraint.

What was she about? At her command, he had married her. Did she intend to shut him out of her life, now and always? Old doubts and suspicions roused anew. Had she taken his name to protect her interests, while disdaining him as too ill-bred and lowborn to be her true consort? Beren frowned. If Guenivere thought to wed him and send him on his way, she was mistaken. Did she not know what happened between husband and wife?

Although Beren had not allowed himself to consider all the ramifications of his nuptials, his reaction to that realization was swift and sure. His body grew hard, his braies tightening, at the very thought of bedding Guenivere. Tonight. *Every night.* He drew in an unsteady breath and tried to master himself, for obviously his bride was not as eager as he.

Did she think to cuckold him? Beren's blood boiled. He had vowed to serve this family, but not to his own disgrace. And did he not deserve an heir? Why should he tender his hard-won lands back to the crown after his death? Although Beren rarely thought about passing on his holdings, now the vague idea became a very real possibility. And he was surprised as a fierce yearning shook him. Suddenly, he wanted a son, and not just with anyone, but with this woman.

The notion of Guenivere round with his child sent heat

surging through him again, but not simply with lust. Pride and hope and long-abandoned dreams pressed in upon him, constricting his chest. For a moment, Beren dared not breathe, so precious was the vision. But before long, he exhaled harshly, dismissing his fantasy. For how would such an idyll come to pass when his bride wanted naught to do with him?

Anger gave him more power than helpless desire, so Beren seized upon it, searching for Guenivere once more. Although the numbers had thinned as villagers left and servants took away cups and food, he did not see her. Several of his knights lingered near the hearth, toasting their liege, but few ladies still graced the room.

Abruptly, Beren felt a prickle on the back of his neck that roused all his awareness. He turned slowly to find not Guenivere, but something else for which he had been searching this hall: an unfriendly face. It was Crispin, an older knight who had long served Brandeth and made no effort to hide his displeasure at the sight of Beren

They stared at each other across the space of tiles. Then, deliberately, Beren stepped toward his old nemesis. Memories of the man's jeers taunted him, but he ignored them, focusing on the here and now, where he would judge the knight anew.

"Well, Crispin?" he asked. "Have you no congratulations for me?"

The elder man nodded curtly. "Of course,... my lord," he said, but his mouth was drawn into a sneer that made his disapproval clear. The two continued to face each other, Beren well aware of the other man's enmity. It was not a new sensation, but he had grown beyond the sting of words. Hadn't he?

"You have done well for yourself, considering your origins," Crispin said. "But perhaps 'twould be better had you rested on your laurels at Edward's side, rather than return here."

"And why is that?" Beren asked.

"You may find that things have changed here."

Beren affected a smile. "But that is to my advantage, is it

not?" he asked, alluding to his own improved circumstances.

Crispin flushed, but did not retreat. "You may think that you have all you ever desired, Berenger, but I doubt that your *wife* shares those sentiments."

Although Beren did not flinch, the barb struck too close to the bone, and Crispin pressed his attack. "For 'tis not the usual wedding night, is it, when the bride retires alone?" he asked, with a smirk.

Beren's temper flared, urging him to have done with this mockery of civility and challenge his old rival. But two things stopped him: consideration for Guenivere and Crispin himself. The man was no longer young, and whatever dreams he had once nurtured were long gone. He remained as he had always been, a bachelor knight with no lands or men of his own, serving a small demesne that was now owned by someone he despised.

"I think that I, too, have grown weary," Beren said. With that, he turned away and headed for the narrow stair that led to the upper chambers. He strode forward with purpose and authority, having well learned the advantages of appearances, but he felt neither.

Although Beren might be the foremost knight in the land and baron of his own great holdings, now he was perilously close to a past very different from his present. And it threatened to drag him back down to places he did not care to go.

Worse yet, he had been married only a few hours, and already it seemed he was estranged from his wife. *Guenivere.* Although Beren still found it hard to believe that they were wed, he could all too readily accept the bitter truth of Crispin's words.

'Tis not the usual wedding night... when the bride retires alone.

CHAPTER TWO

As a knight, Beren had vowed to safeguard all women. Now he wondered bitterly whether that included protecting his own wife from himself. Both anger and pride warred within him, along with lingering remnants of old doubts that urged him not to seek his marital rights, for how could he possibly deserve them?

Beren felt a measure of relief when he reached the top of the stair and saw that the door to the great chamber was open. Perhaps Crispin's attack was as pointless as the dull thud of a bated weapon, and Guenivere was expecting him to join her here. The thought brought Beren's body back to life.

Drawing a deep breath, he sought control over himself and strode to the threshold only to pause in dismay once more. Although there was a fire in the hearth and his things were laid about the room, there was no trace of his wife, nor any signs of her presence.

Beren stepped inside to look more closely, but no woman's hairbrush or personal items were to be found, and the pegs and chests were empty of clothing. His gaze settled upon his own gear, delivered by his squire, and his temper returned in full force. Slamming the lid of the coffer, he stalked out of the room.

In the narrow passage, he hesitated, wondering if his old nemesis had lied to him, and Guenivere remained below. But there was no denying he had not seen her below. So he continued on until he stopped in front of her old chamber. He knew it well, and memories pressed upon him until he pushed them away forcibly. He pushed just as fiercely upon the door, but his efforts had far less effect, for it was barred against him.

Beren told himself that there was some mistake, yet he refused to knock. "Guenivere? Are you there?" he asked. Her name sounded harsh in the quiet, and he swore under his breath. It was this place. If only they were somewhere else. *If only he were someone else...*

"Beren?" He heard her voice through the wood that separated them, and the sound of his true name, not his title, might have been welcome, but for what followed. "What do you want?" she asked.

"I want to retire," Beren said, annoyed at her foolish question. He also was acutely aware that he stood in the narrow passage that ran along the upper rooms, having a conversation that anyone might overhear. On his wedding night. Outside his wife's bedchamber. How could she do this to him? Surely, she knew how it would look. Did she deliberately humiliate him?

"I... had your possessions placed in the great chamber," she said, from behind her oaken shield. Was she so cowardly as to hide from him? Or was she feeling too superior in her bloodlines to open the door to such as him?

"That is very thoughtful of you," Beren said, through gritted teeth. "But I would sleep with my wife."

Silence came from the other side of the door, a long, telling silence. "I really don't think that is wise," she said, at last. She paused, while his blood began to boil anew. "I want to assure you that you need feel no obligation here. You are free to go back to your own demesne and take up your pressing duties."

Right now, the most pressing duty Beren planned to take up was bedding his bride. Whatever doubts he'd had on that score had been driven away by her refusal to grant him an audience, let alone his rights.

Perhaps another man, with less history here, would have accepted her terms. Then again, one look at her, and any man who did not want to exercise his husbandly claims would have to be either blind or insane.

"For now, my duty is here with you," Beren said. "Or do you want your overlord disputing your marriage?"

There came another long pause as she considered that suggestion. "He wouldn't dare," she finally said. "Giffard would not question you, an intimate of the king himself."

It was true. Giffard was a minor landholder, with a few

small fiefs like this one pledged to him. He would make no protest at having one of the most famous knights in the country, with great lands and many men, as an ally. Guenivere was clever and unyielding. The combination infuriated him.

"Open the door, Guenivere," Beren nearly bellowed, his patience running thin.

"That was not part of our bargain."

"Nor was this!" Beren shouted. He could call for an ax and break down the door, of course. He had done no less in war, but he had no wish to do so here, among those who might remember his roots and nod sagely that blood willed out. Instead, turning on his heel, Beren strode away, along the passage and down the stairs, past whispering servants who had been drawn to the spectacle of the great knight brought low by a lady.

It sounded like a poor version of a troubadour's tale, but in such ballads, the cruel woman taunting the knight who loved her was married to someone else. None of those songs and stories told of a husband lusting helplessly after his own wife. And Beren vowed that his would not be the first.

Reining in his emotions, as well as the memories that pressed him, Beren forced himself to think like the warrior he was and focus upon the skills he had long honed. He would need them in order to win the day. Or night.

The moon was with him, lighting the bailey so that Beren could find his way without the aid of a torch. He knew how to move silently when assessing an area, so as to draw little notice, and none noted him now. Although some knights thought 'twas enough to be able to wield lance and sword, Beren had discovered that his most useful weapon was not a strong arm, but an agile mind.

Guenivere wasn't alone in her cleverness. Nor did the trait appear to be governed by birth, for Beren had cultivated it all of his life. Once he had been eager to listen to stories read by another, then he had learned to read and write himself, as did most knights. But he had not stopped there. He had devoured every treatise on knighthood as well as every book he could get his hands on, and he had watched those in command, studying battle tactics, learning and formulating his own strategy.

They were ingrained in him now, so Beren felt fully confident as he walked along the east wall of the castle, gauging his steps and locating his wife's chamber with ease.

She had left a candle burning, perhaps in order to see any attack that came through her barred door or to keep a vigil by it. Instead, she had aided him in finding her window, something he was certain she had not intended. Beren stood beneath it now, smiling grimly as he judged the distance straight up to the softly glowing portal.

He could use a rope, of course, with an axe that would catch neatly upon the stone ledge. But Guenivere would notice such an intrusion, and there was always the chance that she might toss it back down, hopefully without him on it.

Although she might not want to kill her husband, lest she be forced to take another, Beren did not care to test her—or take any injury. Glancing up once more, he thought about using a ladder, another implement utilized in time of siege, but that, too, could be seen and knocked aside.

Dismissing such devices, Beren began to consider the moonlit face of stone with careful deliberation, eyeing each crack and crevice. Soon, he was mentally mapping a route, using that first tiny outcropping for a handhold, then moving swiftly with the seasoned judgment that accompanied experience. Finally, he approached the edifice, knowing that only one manner remained in which to reach the top.

He would climb.

As a child, Beren had been fascinated by the cliffs, spending what few hours time he could spare exploring the jagged outcroppings, the tumbled boulders, and the sheer stone faces, always finding a foothold, always seeking a higher one, always moving upward. Most people deemed it a useless waste of time, but his passion proved the source of his good fortune, and later, the skill many dismissed served him well when assailing another's defenses.

Beren approached the wall, and in the darkness of the deserted bailey, he sought his first hold, carefully, but with confidence. Like so much else in life, a man created his own destiny when climbing. If he thought about falling, he fell. Beren had learned that lesson as a child and put it to good use. He never saw himself failing, only succeeding, and had moved onward, upward, ever striving, unassailed by doubts until he came back here. Today.

Beren pushed that thought aside, for he needed all of his concentration. He had not done this in a long while, his new lands being bereft of anything more than gentle slopes, so his fingers did not have the strength they once had possessed.

But still they held on to the most minute of crevices, and he found his way with ease, the sheer joy of the climb returning with each movement. And when, at least, he reached the window, he felt a sense of triumph unmatched by even the greatest victories in battle.

Pausing just below the ledge, Beren listened, though he heard no sound of Guenivere or her attendants. Hopefully, she was alone. *But not for long.* Putting more weight on his fingers, Beren pushed his body upward until he could see inside.

A candelabra stood at one side of the room, but he could not espy his wife. Was she abed? The thought threatened his will, so he swiftly drew himself up and over the stone, dropping noiselessly inside. The chamber was so much smaller than Beren remembered that for a moment, he wondered whether he was in the right place. Surely, the vast, luxurious room of his youth was not this sparse and simple space?

And yet, something was familiar. He gazed about, slowly recognizing the settle, the hearth, the heavy hangings that hid the bed. The sight of them caused a low sound to escape him. And he realized, too late, that he had just given himself away.

Out of the corner of his eye, Beren saw Guenivere standing at the foot and turning round to gasp in surprise. She was not abed, and Beren didn't know whether he was relieved or disappointed by the discovery.

"Beren! How did you come here?" she asked, not bothering to hide her alarm.

"By the window," Beren said, his expression neutral. He found himself unable to say more as feelings, long buried, pushed to the surface, begging an acknowledgment he would deny. So he stood, unmoving, while she ran past him to put her hands on the ledge, as if to see for herself a ladder or implement of some kind.

"You might have been killed!" she whispered, her hand at her throat and either accusation or fear in her eyes. Beren decided on the former, for Guenivere could ill afford to lose her new spouse. "Why would you dare such a thing?" she demanded. Then she stepped back with a frown, as if struck by a more important concern. "Why have you come?"

Beren met her gaze directly. "I am here to sleep with my wife."

Whatever else she might have felt, her dismay at his reply was obvious. "That was not part of our bargain!" she said again.

"There was no bargain," Beren said. "You ordered me to wed you, and I did. Never did you say that you wanted only a mockery of the holy union."

His words had the desired effect, for Guenivere appeared flustered and bit her lip, an innocent gesture that acted like a kick in his gut. It was an old habit of hers he had seen before, but he reacted quite differently than in the innocence of youth. Now the action drew his attention to her mouth and stirred his body as he watched her draw in a low breath to speak.

"You cannot expect a typical marriage when I will be here and you will be far away, at court or your estates or wherever you will be," she said, waving a hand as if to dismiss his whereabouts.

Beren noted an odd tenor of accusation in her voice that he could not comprehend. But what did he understand of this situation? Nothing beyond his simmering anger and growing frustration, and he had no patience for this sparring of words that could only dredge up things better left buried.

"I expect an heir, Guenivere, and you had better become reconciled to that fact," Beren said bluntly. Ignoring both her startled expression and his own misgivings, he stepped toward her.

She held her ground when he approached her, as he knew she would, tilting her head up in defiance. "What? Would you force yourself upon me, Beren? What happened to your knightly vows, your oath to protect women?"

Beren was tempted to tell her the truth: that her vaunted opinion of knights, based upon the romance stories she so loved, had very little to do with reality. In his long years of fighting, he had seen few men who even remotely resembled those paragons of virtue. And although he had taken his vows more seriously than most, they would not keep him from his own wife.

"What about—"

He cut her off, stopping her words with his mouth, taking her gasp of startled breath as his own. And then his lips touched hers, and he knew nothing, not anger, not disappointment, not the press of old memories, *nothing* except the heady wonder of her taste.

Her lips were softer than roses, and her fragrance far sweeter than crushed petals. Leaning close, Beren lifted his hands toward her shoulders, where they hovered inches from their goal as he hesitated, still certain he did not have the right to touch the lady of the keep. But Guenivere suddenly was within his read. And she was not pushing him away, he realized, with sudden surprise.

Indeed, for someone who had protested his intent loudly, she seemed most compliant. Her lips moved under his, soft and yielding. Beren lifted his head and saw that her lovely neck was arched backward, her eyes closed, and a becoming flush tinted her beautiful cheeks. The sight of her, so obviously struck by desire, stirred both his mind and his body. The kiss he had begun half in anger, to assert himself, now seemed a gift, a precious thing beyond price.

Watching her face with deliberate regard, Beren slowly lowered his hands to her shoulders. Though his fingers met the fine material that gowned her, he could feel her supple form beneath, and for a long moment he simply stared at the picture they made: his tanned, rough hands settled where he never thought them to be, upon the body of Guenivere St. Leger.

The sight was startling in its simplicity, yet so very moving that Beren wasn't sure what was the dream, the past few hours when he had taken her to wife or all the years before, spent in hopeless yearning.

So fierce were the emotions raging through him and so loath was he to break whatever spell lay upon them that Beren paused, savoring the heat beneath his palms, perhaps too long. For while he stood watching her, Guenivere gradually returned to awareness, like a sleeper struggling awake. As she did, her body stiffened, and her lashes lifted to reveal not the dazed wonder that he felt, but the glint of accusation.

"You give the kiss of greeting very well, my lord," she said. "'Tis too bad that your farewells are not as sweet."

Beren stepped back, away from the look in her eyes, away from the past that threatened to engulf him. And yet he felt no better in retreat, for now his hands held nothing. He stared at them, momentarily struck by the loss, then dropped them to his sides.

"Or perhaps you have forgotten that you knew me once ere you won your fame and fortune?" Guenivere asked.

Beren glared at her, willing her not to raise all that he had put behind him. Could they not begin their lives anew, as husband and wife, without dragging up all that was before? "You know full well that I remember you," he said.

"Do I?" she asked. "'Twould be difficult to know for certain since I have heard no word from you, not one single message since you left this place! You never even said good-bye."

Beren stared in surprise at hearing the break in her voice, but she turned away, unable to meet his gaze. With a pang, he realized that try though he might to avoid it, she was taking him back through the years, back here, to the beginning. "What right had I?" he asked harshly.

When she spoke, it was with her back to him and her tone low, as though muffled. "If nothing else, the right of any human being to speak to another."

"'Twas not that simple, and you know it," Beren said. She had never understood. What did she want from him? The truth? Though he willed it not, the answer came to him: He had been afraid he would not have the strength to leave, if she had bid him stay all those years ago.

Yet, why should he let her rouse that old specter? What did he know of her now except her cold proposal that would deny him his rights as her husband?

"Perhaps you would explain it to me," she said. In the ensuing silence, she turned to face him once more, her pale brows lifted in question. But Beren had no explanation, at least none that he wished to give her.

"Then you must leave me to my own assumptions, that you were too eager to leave this place behind and all that it once might have... meant to you. And now you treat with the king himself. I am surprised that you could find your way back to such a small, insignificant plot of land."

So fierce were her emotions that she was trembling. With rage or scorn? Beren did not know, but his temper rose to the challenge. "I came trotting back at your summons, did I not, my lady, like a trained pup? What else would you have me do?" Beren demanded, though he suspected the answer. He was not to touch her, not to look at her, not to have anything of his own in this bloodless contract, except humiliation.

At his outburst, her passion seemed to die, her expression growing still and bleak. "I would have had you return without the summons, without my reminding you of your old vow, or did you forget my father and all that he did for you? Do you know that he died with your name on his lips?"

Guilt assailed him, as was her intention, no doubt, and

Beren ran a rough hand over his face. What could he say, without dredging up all that he kept buried? How to explain such selfishness when it was so far from the knightly ideal she so prized? He said nothing, and she gave him no quarter.

"He was so proud of you! He thought of you as a son, though one long parted from his sire. He would have none say a word against you, nor complain that you did not return," she said. And the implication was clear: Clement had wished to see him, and Beren had failed his old patron.

"I am sorry. 'Twas wrong of me not to come," Beren admitted, swallowing hard against a thickness in his throat. He owed more than he could ever repay to Clement, but he had not made even the meanest effort to do so. He walked to the window and looked out upon the night.

"Even Parzival returned, though 'twas too late, or have you forgotten such trivial things?" Guenivere asked.

At the mention of the character that loomed large in her romantic tales, Beren swung round to face her. "How dare you scold me like one of your errant handmaidens, questioning my honor and fabricating motives for me that suit your own purpose? My reasons for staying away are my own and have nothing to do with ingratitude or false pride."

Guenivere held out her hands, palms upward, in supplication. "Then why?"

What could Beren answer that would not release the floodgates of the past? Yet how could he lie? He settled for a partial truth. "I thought you were wed and would not intrude upon your household."

"If I were married, I probably would not live here," Guenivere said. "And what did my marital status matter?"

Was she really that foolish or arrogant or unseeing? Beren stepped forward. "I did not come because I did not care to see you wed to another." Then he reached out to grasp her shoulder, without hesitation this time. "When I could not have you myself," he said hoarsely.

Then Beren took her mouth, more forcefully than before, staking his claim, possessing her in a way that was far different from his earlier kiss. Perhaps he wanted to drive away the old memories, or his awe and wonder were fading with her close proximity. Or maybe his temper drove him with a mixture of pride and desire.

Whatever the cause, Beren caught her gasp and deepened the kiss, entwining his tongue with hers, invading, exploring, and savoring until his body grew taut and hard. He pulled her to him, and all the fierce, hot yearning of the years rose up in him.

Lifting his hands to her head, Beren fisted them into her long hair, holding her fast as his mouth ravished hers again and again. Finally, he paused for breath, his lips drifting against her silken locks. He whispered her name on a groan, and the memories he had locked away for so long rushed over him. *All for her. 'Twas all for her.*

And now she was his wife. Heat thundered in his blood, throbbing through him in heady victory. In one swift motion, he lifted her in his arms and carried her to the bed, tugging aside the curtains. The covers were laid back, and he placed her against the pale linen, pausing to stare at the picture she made lying there.

It seemed a dream, for so often had he imagined her thus before he had put aside such fancies. Now he would revel in the sight. Her blond hair, gleaming in the candlelight, lay spread upon the pillow, inviting him to lay his head down beside hers. Her body, slender and womanly, drew his attention, and for the first time in his life he allowed himself to take the measure of her breasts with his gaze, the gentle slopes, the clear skin that rose above her gown.

Beren feasted upon the view there and below where lay the indentation of her waist, the curve of her hips, and her long legs, more visible now as she lay prone, ending in trim ankles and narrow feet encased in thin slippers.

My wife. Beren trembled at the knowledge. He let his gaze wander at will, then slowly he brought it back to her face, pale and beautiful and beloved. He could not divine what he saw there: sweetness and a kind of dazed aspect that could be attributed to desire. But paramount was a wariness, a guarded look that had never appeared in his dreams. He held his breath, dreading her protest.

Instead of waiting for it, Beren leaned over her, intending to stop whatever words she would put between them, but he halted at the touch of her hand against his chest. Her slender fingers burned through his tunic like fire, but there was no denying her intention: to ward him off.

Beren stayed where he was, watching as she bit her lip. He swallowed a groan, for he wanted to bite her lips himself, soft nibbles that led to a voracious feeding beyond his wildest imaginings..

"Such was Parzival's regard for his wife that he did not think of making love to her for three nights after the wedding," Guenivere said, referring once more to her favorite tale.

"Too late, for I have already thought of it," Beren said. He had dreamed of it endless nights long ago, forever it seemed, until his blood flamed and his body burned...

"Parzival—"

Beren blew out a breath in exasperation. "I am not Parzival, no matter how you would wish me to be!" he said. Riled beyond endurance, he rose to his feet. "Nor an I Lancelot nor Gawain nor any legendary figure of the romances!"

And finally, after all the anger and accusations and speeches of a tiring night, the one thing that stopped Beren from bedding his own wife was this terrible reminder: she knew what he was—and would never accept him.

CHAPTER THREE

Guenivere busied herself sewing. She had continued with her usual tasks this morning, such as meeting with the cooks, while ignoring the surprised glances of the servants and the tittering of her handmaidens. They dared not question her directly, but she cringed when she heard their whispered speculations concerning her wedding night.

The household was rife with rumor about how the great knight had climbed up the side of the very keep to enter through her window. The men boasted of their new lord's boldness and daring, while the women sighed at the romantic feat. Only Guenivere knew that romance had nothing to do with it.

She took a deep, shaky breath, trying not to think of how Beren had kissed her, or worse yet, the way he had touched her, carrying her to bed and eyeing her like a starving villein would a feast. Apparently, men were more interested in such things than she had ever imagined. How else could one barge in and demand intimacies from a virtual stranger?

It was her own fault for summoning him here, Guenivere knew, yet she had acted out of desperation. After her father's death, the neighbors had swarmed like a pack of carrion crows, eager to dine on her small holding.

Yet she refused to hand over her inheritance to any of them. Not many cared for the windswept crags that made up her lands, and fewer still would appreciate its raw beauty. The place was bred into your bones, and Guenivere wanted no absent lord who would disdain her heritage, abandoning all responsibilities except to exact payment.

But she was no fool, and she knew she could not hold off forever the men who deemed the world their own and would deny one woman her small holding. Sooner or later, her overlord would have stepped in, awarding both her and the castle to whomever he pleased. Guenivere would have been forced to marry someone not of her own choosing, a man who might not have liked her hone, who might have taken her away from Brandeth and the people who had long served her family.

That terror, more than any other, had made her swallow her pride and beg for help. And who else to give it to her except Beren—knighted by her father? Had he not sworn allegiance in return?

Still, it had taken all her courage to send for him, and even Guenivere had not been bold enough to specify her need, for fear that he would never consider it. Worse yet, there was always the possibility that he might turn her request over to someone else, another lord or the king himself, leaving her situation just as dire as before.

But Beren had come, and he had agreed, and foolishly, Guenivere had deemed her problems over. She had thought that the great Sir Brewere, having fulfilled his oath, would be eager to go on to more important business and finer accommodations. Why would she have imagined otherwise when he had acted as if he hardly recognized her?

Yet Guenivere had known him at once, though he was greatly changed. Indeed, such was the power of his appearance that her knees had nearly given way. He was not the skinny youth who had left Brandeth, but a man, full grown and fleshed out hard with muscle and strength that she had felt in his touch, and Guenivere's pulse skittered at the memory.

Even when young, Beren had never appeared soft, yet his face now held the aspect of a fearsome warrior, and for a moment, Guenivere had quailed before him. She had searched for glimpses of the boy she had known in his dark eyes, but found them shuttered and steeled herself accordingly. If she secretly had dreamed of another sort of greeting, it had gone the way of all her other dreams, and she accepted his blunt acknowledgment as a harbinger of what was to come: vows made by duty.

What else did she expect when she had forced this marriage upon him? Guenivere felt a prick of guilt. She had pressed Beren, seizing what she thought was her only chance, though he had appeared loathe to wed her.

At the thought Guenivere lifted her chin. Who, then, could blame her for seeking the solace of her chamber? And who would have thought that the solemn, distant knight intended to join her there?

The memory sent a flood of crimson to her cheeks, and Guenivere ducked her head in an attempt to hide her embarrassment. She did not want her handmaidens to notice her blush and comment upon it, and she was glad that she had sent the overly inquisitive Alys to fetch a draught. Unfortunately, just as the thought passed through her mind, the girl was back, breathlessly reporting that Lord Brewer had arisen and was breaking his fast.

Guenivere's hand jerked as her pulse quickened again, but she showed no other outward sign of having heard. Whatever Beren was about, she was not interested. But Alys, who seemed far younger than fifteen years, would not be discouraged by her mistress' lack of attention. She began to carry on at great length about the "new lord."

"He is not lord here, really, but an overlord who will soon be away," Guenivere said.

"Off to far places and magnificent castles to fight for his lady," Alys said with a sigh, while Guenivere grimaced. She had no idea what battle Alys could imagine being conducted on her behalf.

"Surely, there has never been the like of such a man, tall and broad-shouldered and dark of hair and eye," Alys said. "Why, just the sight of him is enough to cause any maiden to swoon. And if that were not enough, he is a knight and a baron and a companion of Edward himself. 'Tis almost as if an intimate of King Arthur's round table came to life!"

"I thought I asked you to stop reading romances," Guenivere said, snapping her thread sharply. She lifted her head to send both girls a quelling glance for their habits.

When would they ever learn? The romance stories were

fantasy, as were the ballads sung by the troubadours to willing audiences.

Despite the prevalence of certain plots, knights did not really commit adultery with queens and ladies or they would be castrated by their lord. There were no "courts of love," unless they existed in exotic foreign lands, for here men did not make vows that were judged by ladies. Most were too busy seeking their own glory to give a thought to any female. And those women who hoped otherwise were only asking for heartache. Guenivere pulled on the thread again—hard.

"But, my lady," Alys protested. "How can you ask us to forgo our only pleasure? The stories give us a glimpse of the excitement to be had at court and beyond, of places far away and handsome princes! You have to admit there is little enough chivalry to be found here."

Or anywhere, Guenivere thought. But before she could speak, Alys sighed deeply. "If only some great knight like Sir Brewere would come for me!"

"Beren didn't come for me. I sent for him," Guenivere said, exasperated. Although she disliked speaking of her marriage, it was better that the girl know the truth than babble on like a dreamy-eyed maiden fed on fables. *Like the girl Guenivere had been.*

Guenivere frowned. Her father, having loved the Arthurian stories, had dubbed her accordingly and encouraged her interest in her namesake and the heroic legends of the past. In truth, Guenivere had needed little urging, for she had devoured the romances, reading them aloud to others and investing all her hopes in nothing but a bit of ink and parchment, a tale told by a fool.

But with age had come wisdom and, thankfully, the ability to tell the difference between fact and fabrication. Knights did not fall in love with maidens at first sight, nor become so consumed with love that they forgot all else. *'Twas the maidens they were more likely to forget.*

"Lest you twist the truth to suit your fancy, Alys, I might remind you that until my summons, Sir Brewere had no intention of returning to Brandeth. And he married me only because I held him to the oath he made to my father," Guenivere said, bitter though the words might be to speak.

"But how can you claim so after last night?" Alys asked.

Guenivere's face flamed, and she ducked her head once more, as if intent upon her handiwork. "What do you mean?" she murmured. Surely, no one knew of the kisses Beren had stolen—or the way they had made her feel.

"Why, 'tis said that so enamored was he, that he called the very clouds to his bidding and soared through the air to your window to enter your bower."

Guenivere grimaced at the obvious falsehood, but it did not matter what people said. Whether they claimed he sprouted wings and flew or drifted on the breeze or crawled like a spider up the stone, she knew it was a feat that only Beren could have accomplished. She had watched him climb years ago, her heart in her throat as he seemed to dangle in nothingness only to emerge at the top of a crag, laughing and triumphant.

The memory seared her, tempting her to revisit others, but Guenivere hardened herself with more recent recollections. Only Beren could turn everything, even a seemingly impenetrable wall, to his advantage. And only Beren would expect to take up just where he had left off. But Guenivere was not so quick to forget the intervening years. Nor did she intend to let this man she no longer knew into her life—and her bed.

Guenivere flushed anew, but remained resolved. Last night she had managed to stay him. He had slept on a fur before the fire, completely clothed, while she had lain atop the bedclothes, wide-eyed and wary. When she finally had drifted off, it was to awaken with a start, bewildered and angry at his presence in her chamber. Yet there he had been, and she wondered just how long he intended to stay.

What if he remained this day, as well? What of this night? Guenivere felt her pulse pound in a rhythm born of panic, not excitement. Or so she told herself. Obviously, she could not count upon Beren's disinterest. Nor could she lock herself away, for she did not want him to shout outside her door. *Or break it down.* Guenivere shuddered at the thought of defying the man Beren had become: strong, confident, and lethal looking.

What, then, could she do? Fleeing was out of the question. Travel was too difficult, and she had no safe haven except her own home, a keep that now belonged to *him*. Guenivere swallowed that bitter draught and tried to concentrate. Her recollections of the night were a haze of recriminations, threats, and the overriding fear that he would press her to submit. *And that she would succumb.*

Unbidden, the memory of his kisses returned, and Guenivere shivered, though she felt suffused with heat. How different they had been from her girlish imaginings! She had thought only a touch of the lips was involved, not a melding of mouths and tongues, not a fusing of breath and of souls... But perhaps Beren felt no such connection. He was a stranger to her now and refused even to excuse his long absence.

That knowledge drove away any lingering warmth, and Guenivere hardened herself once more. She had spent many hours of the night wondering why Beren could not admit that he had forgotten all who dwelt at Brandeth. Instead, he had hedged his words and lashed out. And as for his claim that he had not wanted to see her married to another, Guenivere would have laughed had she the heart.

If Beren had wanted her for himself, he had only to claim her at any time since she had first set eyes upon him. In that moment, long ago, Guenivere had vowed to herself that he was the stuff of her dreams, the other half of herself, *her destiny.* But such a man would never have left her, or else he would have returned, triumphant, to sweep her off her feet.

Guenivere made a low sound of disgust, for now she was lapsing into the language of the romances, a foolishness she had thought long past. Unfortunately, just the sight of Beren seemed to send her slipping into her old habit, for had she not brought up Parzival last night? Guenivere winced as she remembered her words. *Such was Parzival's regard for his wife that he did not think of making love to her for three nights after the wedding.*

It was nonsense, for nothing could be farther from her marriage than the union of the legendary hero and his wife. Yet when she had quoted the tale to him, Beren had left her, angry at the comparison between himself and the knight. Had he been reminded of the lack of chivalry in his behavior, or had something else turned him away? Guenivere did not know, but she hoped the words would work as well again, if she needed them.

And after three nights, then what? Guenivere trembled and told herself that Beren would be gone by then, off again to his adventures, leaving Brandeth behind as before.

When Beren was still in residence come supper, Guenivere felt her nerves stretched taut. She had avoided him all of the day, even going so far as to take the main meal in her chamber. Still, she had hardly been able to swallow a bite, for fear he would search her out, bearding her there, especially after Alys breathlessly reported his absence at the high table.

Where had he eaten, and when? Guenivere found herself wondering and worrying only to chide herself for slipping into old patterns again. More likely, the simple fare at Brandeth no longer appealed to his more sophisticated tastes. And 'twas not only the food that could be so described, Guenivere thought bitterly.

She frowned, pushing aside such thoughts to consider what Beren was about. According to Alys, he had shown little interest in the keep or its outbuildings, preferring to remain closeted with the old bailiff, going over the books. The idea of another judging her work here annoyed Guenivere, for what did Beren know of this place anymore? Should he question her management, she vowed to give him a tongue-lashing.

Guenivere stilled at her place by the hearth, seized by the notion of using her tongue for other than speech. She glanced at the chamber door, fearful she would be tempted to explore further these new avenues... Already, twilight was gathering outside her window. Would he come, or not? Guenivere trembled, though she knew not which outcome she most dreaded.

And then he was there, opening her door as though he had full use of her chamber and herself. Guenivere drew in a sharp breath and glanced up at him, but his dark eyes were shuttered, and she could read nothing in his expression.

Would he suddenly seize her? Scold her for avoiding him? Guenivere set her shoulders and told herself she feared no man, least of all Beren Brewere, lord or no.

"I looked over your accounts today," he said. "You have done well."

Surprised at his words, Gueniverc glanced up and tried not to stare. Would she ever grow accustomed to the sight of him? His dark hair swept back, thick and smooth, nearly to his shoulders, which now were broad and wide and strong, as was the rest of him. He had always been tall, but now his body had grown to match his height, all hard with muscle that was visible through the linen of his tunic. Guenivere swallowed and tore her gaze away.

"Did you eat?" she asked.

"Yes," he said. And then he astounded her by laughing, though it was not a lighthearted sound. "You might not be pleased to know this, but since neither of us were at the high table, all of your people think we were up here, engaged in newly wedded bliss."

Guenivere swung round with a gasp. "But, I—" she sputtered before turning away. "Did you eavesdrop?"

"Nay. I did not have to," Beren said. "Brandeth is buzzing with rumors and speculation."

They will die down, if you would but leave, Guenivere thought. Aloud, she said, "Yes, I heard some of it myself, most notably how you hopped on a cloud to fly through my window."

Beren laughed, and this time the sound was soft and low and so compelling that Guenivere had to use all her will to remain still. "Apparently, your unusual talent for climbing has been forgotten," she said.

Silence met her comment, so long and all encompassing that finally, Guenivere turned to look at him again, only to find that he had wrapped his cloak about him and lay upon the floor, his back to her. Obviously, his brief interest in her charms had faded once more. Guenivere struggled with a sharp sense of disappointment that bordered on hurt before convincing herself she ought to be relieved instead.

Then she rose to her feet and sought her bed, pulling the drapes close around her and shutting Beren out. But it seemed as if the habit of long years returned, for though he might be out of sight, he was never far from her mind.

Beren tried to sleep, but it would not come. He had made his bed on harder, colder spots, but none more painful to both body and spirit. He had spent the day closeted with the bailiff, concentrating on the management of the demesne and changing the subject whenever the old man started to reminisce.

But those distractions were over, and Beren winced as the scent of roses wafted over him, rousing his blood to a fever pitch. Although he prided himself on his good sense, it appeared to have fled, for why else would he ache for a woman with whom he could not bear to talk? How had he wed the one woman who would not have him? And why was she still here, unmarried after all these years?

Beren seized upon that question, worrying it until he could not let it go. Had he not heard that she was betrothed at one time? Without examining too closely that memory, he wondered what had happened. Had the man died or been found wanting? The more Beren thought about it, the more tense he became. Finally, he rolled over and spoke aloud into the dimness.

"What happened to your betrothed? Why did you not marry?" Beren asked, his voice harsh and accusing as he rose up on one arm. For a long moment, he thought she was asleep or feigning so and would not answer. Angry, he felt like striding over to rouse her, but he knew that was not a good idea. He shouldn't even be looking at her bed, he thought grimly.

Although he had tried to forget everything to do with the lady of Brandeth, Beren knew that no matter how long he lived, he would ever remember the sight of those curtains parting. Whatever he thought, he wasn't expecting that, and he held his breath in tense anticipation.

When at last Guenivere was revealed in the dim light of the fire, he could see she was fully clothed, yet still he felt hot desire run rampant through him, for there she was, kneeling upon the covers, her hair loose and flowing...

"'Twas broken off," she said. As if that marked the end of her comments on the topic, she reached up to draw the curtains once more. Beren's heart lurched, as if it would leap from his chest in order to stay her hand.

"By whom?" he asked, hoarsely.

"By me." Her eyes downcast, she looked as if she did not care to speak of it. But suddenly, Beren had to know. What had the man done?

"Why?" he demanded, ready, despite all, to battle on her behalf.

With a sigh, Guenivere swung her legs round to sit on the edge of the bed. "As I grew older, Father became concerned because I had shown no marked partiality for any who sought my hand," she explained in a flat voice, still without looking at him. "He thought to force a decision from me by betrothing me to William of Langbane. Rather than cause trouble for my sire, I thought that I should accept." Although her words rang true, Beren's gut churned.

"I believed that I could do it," she said. She paused, taking an interest in a decorative cord that dangled from the drape beside her, rubbing it between her fingers as thought it would give her comfort or strength before dropping it abruptly. "But I finally told Father that I could not in all good conscience commit myself to the marriage when I felt I would fail William as a wife.

Beren swallowed a protest, for Guenivere had never failed

at anything. And he knew of no man who was worthy of her, *not even himself.*

"Since my father cared very much for my mother, he was reluctant to compel me into a loveless union, especially when it would take me away from him." Finally, she met Beren's gaze with a rather defiant look. "That was the end of the betrothal. William was gracious about it and married Elizabeth Trowford a few months later."

At her simple explanation, Beren felt a euphoria beyond all reason. He was glad that there had been no love between the two, and fast on the heels of his elation came a surge of possessiveness. At that moment, Beren wanted nothing more than to go to her, take her in his arms, and make her forget every other man she had ever known.

"What of you? Why have you not wed?"

Guenivere's question stayed his rampaging impulses and scattered them like the fancies they were. He pulled his cloak about him tightly.

"Mayhap I was a bachelor knight too long to change my ways," Beren muttered. Then he turned over once more, shutting her out, lest he be laid bare before her.

CHAPTER FOUR

Beren stood at the doors of the hall, staring out to the sea and wondering what he was doing here when it was the last place he wanted to be. He ought to leave. There were no obstacles to his doing so, especially not the wishes of his wife. And yet, something held him here, whether the past or the future, he wasn't sure.

But he was accomplishing nothing, reluctant as he was to come to terms with his history, while other duties waited for him at his own demesne. Yet that place no longer seemed his home. Instead, he had a sinking suspicion that his destiny lay here, with his roots. Beren shook his head with a grunt of denial.

"Are you still here?" As if his own thoughts were being voiced aloud, Beren heard the question ring out. But it came from Crispin, who was standing nearby by with a sneer on his lips.

"This is my keep now, Crispin. Would you try to rout me from it?" Beren asked. His patience worn down to nothing by his bride, he was in no mood for the older knight's taunts. For a moment, he thought Crispin might challenge him, and his own hand moved to the hilt of his sword. But the other man only crossed his arms over his chest.

"Nay, for I'm sure you'll be home soon enough," he said. "Linger if you must, though for what purpose, I wonder? No one remembers you, and those few who do wish they did not."

Beren might have disputed the claim, for the people of Brandeth treated him with courtesy, if not enthusiasm, he realized, with some surprise. As though in proof, another of the keep's knights strode by, calling a greeting.

"Good day, my lord!" the younger man said, adding a welcoming gesture that did not appeared feigned. And with a nod, Beren acknowledged the man's passing. Then he turned back to Crispin, his brows lifted in query.

"Those who don't know you may bow and scrape to Edward's lackey, but no one wants you here," the old knight practically snarled. "I told you that things have changed, so you might as well be gone! And lest you think the lady of Brandeth still pines for your presence, she came to her senses long ago and curses your name as well as any of the others!"

With that, Crispin turned on his heel and marched away, though he had not been given leave to go by his lord. Beren stared after him, too stunned to dispute his exit.

Guenivere pining for him? Beren shook his head, unable to believe it, but he knew Crispin was not clever enough to spin such a lie. Despite his best judgment, hope leapt to life within his chest, and Beren knew that he must discover the truth ere he left Brandeth. And there was only one way to find out.

He must ask Guenivere.

Although Beren avoided dinner again, that night he took supper in the hall, and he wondered what had kept him away. Besides Crispin, who sent him dark looks, no one else seemed to harbor ill feelings toward him. And if some older resident bid him recall the past, Beren simply changed the subject. 'Twas an easier task than trying to explain away the absence of his bride, for he suffered a few good-natured, if ribald, comments concerning her condition.

Beren paid no heed, enduring even more when he left the table early to seek his wife's chamber. Ever since his conversation with Crispin, he had been eager to confront her. But his steps lagged as old doubts assailed him, and he knew the past he denied might rise up to smite him.

Still, he could not bring himself to leave Brandeth without knowing this one truth, and so continued to her chamber. There he found her seated on the settle before the hearth, staring into the flames as if the weight of the world sat upon her shoulders. And in that moment, Beren realized that he had done her ill.

She had asked for his aid, and though providing his name, he had thought of nothing except his pride, ignoring her woes and worries, the burden she carried of her father's loss and the responsibility of holding her lands together. Even if she cared naught for him, Guenivere deserved more than his petulance.

Beren approached her slowly. This time, when he dropped to his knee, 'twas not a gesture born of duty, but heartfelt. Memories nudged at him, but he ignored them and drew a deep breath. "How may I serve you, lady?" he asked, bowing his head.

To Beren's astonishment, Guenivere burst into tears. Confused, he watched helplessly, then lifted a hand toward her, though he was not certain how to provide comfort. But she moved out of his reach before he could touch her. Rising to her feet, she dashed away her tears.

"Do not mock me!" she said, turning upon him. The passion that she usually withheld glowed like a brand, stunning Beren with its intensity. "Would you destroy everything that I once held dear?"

"What is it? What have I done?" Beren asked, bewildered yet aroused by this woman, alight with an inner flame he had never witnessed before. She was grown now, and not only in body, and Beren's blood heated in acknowledgment.

She glared at him, a flush rising in her cheeks, her fury evident. "You? You have done nothing, of course!" Then, as swiftly as it had come upon her, the rage faded away, leaving her looking so lost and forlorn that Beren felt his chest constrict.

"I am at fault," she whispered. "For I placed all my hopes and dreams and love in the hands of another, who failed me." She turned away from him, hid her face in her hands, and wept once more.

Beren stood staring in shock, for until today, he had never seen Guenivere in tears. In her youth she had been too contented, too composed to cry over slights to her happy existence. And as a grown woman she had seemed too cool and remote to be touched by strong emotion. But there was no denying her distress.

Something inside Beren roused to life, and feelings long buried rose to match her own. Who had done this to her? Moved beyond all caution, he stepped forward and took her by the shoulders, drawing her back against him. but the comfort that he intended was hampered by his own anger and jealousy.

"Tell me who stole your dreams. Who failed you? Who," Beren began, nearly choking on the words, "spurned your love?"

To his surprise, she laughed, a low gurgle that sounded more like despair than mirth. "Know you not, Beren? Then you must be as ignorant as Parzival."

Beren opened his mouth to protest the mention of the legendary hero, then shut it again as he realized the meaning of her words. He drew in a sharp breath of both pain and disbelief. "If you think 'twas I, then I can only beg your forgiveness for any broken faith."

"Broken faith?" she asked, as if amused by his choice of words. "Nay, you made no promise to me, ere you left. 'Twas my own fault for foolishly clinging to hope for far too long."

Beren's fingers tightened over her shoulders as his world shook, destroying not only his recent assumptions, but perceptions born of many long years.

"When I heard of your knighting, I rejoiced in your good fortune," Guenivere said. "At last, you had what you most desired! 'Twas your dream, and mine, too, for I had hoped that once knighted, you would ask for my hand." She gave a brittle laugh that wrenched Beren's heart, and he bowed his head to touch her own.

"But when Father returned, 'twas without you. You went away, he said, to earn a name for yourself." Beren opened his mouth to protest, for it was money that he hoped to earn, possessing none. But before he could speak, Guenivere continued, as though unable to stop the flow of words once begun.

"For a long time, I waited for a message. I knew that you could not read, but still I hoped for some sign, and I plagued each passing minstrel and packman, begging for news of you. There came no word, and I knew not where you were. I wrote letters to you nonetheless, planning to send them once I learned your whereabouts. but the months passed, and then the seasons passed, and my hope grew dim."

She paused to draw a ragged breath that made her slender back shudder against him. "'Then, at last, we began to hear of your deeds, of a knight who had won many tournaments, who journeyed far, gaining great renown. Father was thrilled and proud, but my happiness was tempered by selfishness. Had you forgotten me? Would you ever return?

Beren felt her pain, as well as his own, dredged up beyond all hope of reburial. He slid his hands down to her waist, pulling her to him as if to deny all that had happened.

"I never shared my hopes with my father, and eventually he began to press me to marry. I understood his concerns for the future, and yet, I balked, unwilling to surrender the last shred of my dreams. And though outwardly I had given up waiting, at night I imagined you would ride up to Brandeth to claim your lady."

Beren's arms tightened around her even as she uttered the accusations he could not deny. "And that is why you broke the betrothal," he said. Although Beren knew he ought to feel guilty, instead he was glad that she felt no love for another. And he rejoiced to learn that she had waited for him so long.

"I didn't intend to stay away," he said. He drew in a deep breath and prepared to face the past, or at least the part of it that was Guenivere. And, oh, how much of it she was! "At first I sought only to stay alive in battle. Then, when the fighting ended, I could think of little except becoming a proper knight."

Beren paused to carefully choose his words. "But, as I soon discovered, 'tis not the occupation of a poor man, a small fact that is little mentioned in the romances." He hesitated again, unwilling to admit the truth at last, though he knew she deserved it. "I needed money not only to live, to feed myself, but for mail and weapons, and most expensive of all, a good destrier."

"But Father would have—"

Beren interrupted her with a grunt. "Clement had done enough. 'Twas up to me to make my fortune." He drew in another deep breath. "I could not return to you penniless, a beggar at the door of the castle, raised up to knighthood, but with nothing to offer you."

Beren felt Guenivere stir within the circle of his arms, but he held her fast, finding himself loath to let her go—or to face her.

"All I wanted was *you!*" she protested.

Beren shook his head sadly. "But I would have been no measure of a knight, or even a man, had I come to you with naught."

"What nonsense males take into their heads," Guenivere muttered.

Beren smiled at her outrage, even though he knew he could have done nothing else. "Clement suggested I make a living by tourneying, and I managed to do well for myself," he said. "I defeated many others, winning the value of their horse and mail in ransom, and I began to hoard a tidy sum."

"And what amount would have been enough?" Guenivere asked, a trace of bitterness in her tone. "When would you have amassed enough to return?"

Beren didn't reply, for he was not sure of the answer himself. Never for a moment had he forgotten her. Guenivere had been with him always, his anchor and his talisman, the reason for all that he did.

And yet, even when Edward chose him, Beren had been no more than a bachelor knight, without lands to call his own. Would he have come back to claim Brandeth? By what right? So he always put off his return, thinking that he must do more, have more, *be more.*

He swallowed against the tightening of his throat. "Lords began to notice me and take me into service, until finally Edward himself, who loves the tournaments, bid me join him in his war against Wales. 'Twas then that I heard of your betrothal."

His anger at the news had sent him pounding into battle, forging through the ranks of the enemy like a lance, earning him a renown that he no longer sought. And when finally the fighting was over and Edward had gifted him with lands, Beren had imagined her already wed to another. He had buried his hopes, along with a good part of himself.

"And why didn't you come for me then, when you heard of my betrothal?" Guenivere asked.

"We were headed into battle," Beren said. But there was more to it, as they both knew, and he could not tender that excuse. He blew out a low breath. "What right had I to interfere with your happiness?"

"And so you left me to a stranger, absolving yourself of any concern, without even wondering if I were well and content?" Guenivere asked, her voice rising.

"Neither did you send any of the letters you claim to have written, to commend me or command me or inform me that you still remembered my name!" Beren countered.

"I had my pride!" Guenivere said.

"As did I!"

The room fell into silence then, until at last Guenivere spoke again. "So we both suffered for it," she said. "And now it is too late."

"Is it?" Beren asked. How could he believe that when he could rest his chin upon her bright hair, inhale her sweet fragrance, and feel her supple body pressed against his own? As he turned her in his arms, reveling in the miracle of her closeness, all the years fell away. And if any doubts lingered from his long exile, Beren ignored them in the rush of joy that swept through him.

When she faced him, he lifted her chin and saw her sparkling lashes, wet with tears. Kissing them away, Beren let his mouth wander over her beloved features, brushing against her finely arched brows, her pale cheeks, her lips...

When Guenivere met his mouth with her own, tentative but eager, Beren felt his body jerk to life. He groaned, bringing her closer even as her arms slipped around his neck. And then somehow he was carrying her to the bed, laying her among the linens. But this time, when he stood over her, she pulled him down to join her.

Beren needed no urging as he moved over her. He had waited too long for this moment, hardly daring to hope. And when she looked up at him, no longer cool or accusing, but tender and yearning, the last of the walls he had erected between them crumbled.

"Guenivere," he whispered. He was consumed by awe and desire and the love he had kept so carefully guarded all these years. He leaned over her, taking in the vision of her beneath him, and every sight, every sound, every touch was a feast for his starving senses.

When he lifted his hand, he hesitated for a long moment before lowering it to the shining length of her hair. The bright strands were like silk under his fingers, rivaled only by the softness of her skin when he stroked her slender throat.

"Beren." Guenivere spoke his name softly, but with an underlying urgency that set his blood thundering. Then she pulled his head down to hers, and he kissed her with the mixture of ardor and adoration that flowed through him, drawing her breath into himself.

Her kiss was so much more than he had ever dared imagine that Beren might have been content to continue it all night long, dwelling on the lips that had haunted his dreams since childhood. But Guenivere moved against him, sending heat to his loins and spurring him on.

So he touched her, running his hands through her hair, along her side, and over her slender hips. With a groan, he lifted her to him, feeling the press of her against his hardness, and he knew a desire to lift her gown and bury himself inside her. But he fought for control, his love for her slowing his pace.

Raising his head, Beren looked into her face and saw wonder and passion, the heady reflection of his own emotions.

Everything he had ever wanted was here and now. Taking her hand, Beren kissed her fingers.

"My lady, will you have me?" he asked. "As your husband in truth?" His lips upon her knuckles, he held her gaze as he waited for her answer.

"Yes, Sir Knight," she said. And she smiled, though her eyes shone and her voice trembled.

Loosing a sigh of pleasure, Beren carefully stripped off her gown, each inch of exposed flesh a precious find that he must worship with his eyes and his touch and his lips. At last she lay naked before him, slender and white, but he had only a moment to feast his gaze upon her, for she tugged at his tunic until he tossed it over his head.

Then she sat up to press kisses along his chest. Beren groaned, catching her against him, and they both sank back upon the linens as he dragged away his braies.

The feel of her skin against his own was almost more than he could bear, and he shuddered, seized by both a driving need for completion and a desire to remain thus forever, body to body and heart to heart. But Guenivere was sliding against him, a siren call he could not forbear, and he moved over her, claiming the prize he had spent his life trying to win.

When at last he entered her, Beren felt as though he were home at last. And it had nothing to do with the lands granted him by the king or with the windswept crags of Brandeth. Here, with this woman, he found peace and challenge, beauty and wit, the past and the future.

Beren wanted to speak, to put some of what he felt into words, but they were beyond him as he strove past her maidenhead. She cried out then, and he did his best to soothe her, plying her with pleasure until she called out once more, in celebration, rather than loss. And Beren joined her.

Overwhelmed by the force of his release, he was slow to recover his wits. But gradually Beren came to his senses, rolling to his side, so he would not crush her slender form, and pulling her close. Now was the time to unburden himself, to tell her all that was in his heart, yet even as his arms tightened around her, Beren heard the deep and even breathing that told him she slept.

As well she should, he thought, drawing a covering over her. He was weary as well, but loath to sleep, lest he wake and find it all a dream—both his marriage and its consummation. So he held her to him, but even in his bliss, Beren felt the nudge of old doubts, the bane of his existence, and his heart beat feverishly until his body roused to full awareness.

He realized that once was not enough, that he needed Guenivere again, to drive away all uncertainty, to assure himself that she was his, now and forever. His hands began moving over her, exploring every part of her until she awoke, already dazed with desire.

Still, Beren took his time, marveling at each gasp of delight as he learned what she most craved even as he fed his own excitement. And the force of their passion pushed away the darkness until at last, exhausted, he found his rest.

CHAPTER FIVE

Beren's first hint that all might not be well was waking up alone. For a long moment, he thought his memories of the night before might be phantoms of some long-ago dream. But the scent of their lovemaking lingered in the air, as did the imprint of her body beside him.

Had she left to groom herself privately or attend her duties? Beren tried to convince himself such was the case, but it was barely dawn. And strive as he might, he knew he could not account himself a good judge of Guenivere's feelings, else he would have been here years ago.

By what right? Beren wondered, and the doubts he thought vanquished assailed him anew. For all the passion that raged between them, Guenivere had never spoken of her love aloud. Perhaps now she regretted what had happened between them, her absence speaking more eloquently than the words that were so difficult between them. Beren exhaled harshly, all of his pent-up emotions rising to seek an outlet. He rubbed a rough hand across his face, as if to change his features—or *himself*.

Suddenly, all that he had been denying, all the bitter realities of his youth, came back to him. Things he had thought banished from his memory returned to beset him: the smell of animals and hopelessness, the gnaw of hunger and cold, a weariness of body and mind beyond anything he had ever known in battle.

Beren broke out in a sweat, eager to escape, but there was nowhere to go, no place to hide. And he was done taking the coward's way, retreating from his own history and burying the past. Pushing aside the blankets, he rose to his feet.

It was time to face everything.

Dressing swiftly, Beren slipped through the keep where only a few residents were stirring and stepped out into the brisk cool of morning. He took a deep breath and felt the ocean air enter his lungs, tangy and fine. And instead of ignoring his delight, he reveled in it, for he had missed the scent of the sea, just as he had missed Guenivere. How had he come to give up so much of himself? And for what?

Beren walked through the bailey and out the gate toward the village. The past was all around him, and he let it return. His birth was clouded in shadow, as were his first years: a darkness of hunger and want and toil, relieved only by sporadic forays to the cliffs that were his only solace.

The thought led Beren there, and his breath caught as he let himself look upon the steep crags, more beautiful to him than the greenest of rolling hills that were now his own. Perilous many called them, and those who did shrank from the jumble of boulders that led to the sharp inclines moving straight up.

To be sure, Beren had a healthy respect for the cliffs, especially when they were made all the more deadly by cold and rain. And yet, he had been born with a fascination for the rock, with the look and feel of it, and with the conquering of it by skill and the force of his own will.

He had found something of worth in his bleak world, that of a poor orphan boy of unknown parentage taken in by the brewer and his brood. He wrinkled his nose, for he still hated the reek of ale and would drink wine or water when he could. He ought to have been grateful, at least that's what everyone said, for he could have been taken for a villein and a life of mind-numbing, backbreaking labor.

The brewer was not particularly kind, and Beren had been beaten often enough for "dallying" on the cliffs instead of working. Yet he could not forsake them. Somehow he had found new energy on the stone and expansion of mind and spirit that renewed his tired body. And it was this passion that had raised him up from a short and weary life.

For one day he had climbed higher than ever before, something inside him driving him onward and upward until at last he had reached the top and stood staring out from the dizzying height. From there it seemed that he could see the entire world, the sea stretching out into infinity, the line of the cliffs and the coast, and far off, in the distance, a multitude of armed men heading toward Brandeth.

That day, Beren had sounded the alarm and the lord of the castle, Clement himself, had plucked him from the sodden despair of his home with the brewers and made him a squire, altering his destiny forever. Many, openly or not, disapproved of this sudden elevation of a ragged boy, little more than a villein, to a coveted position at the lord's side. But not Clement's daughter.

Guenivere immediately befriended him, and announcing that a squire must be learned, she saw it as her duty to teach him. Although younger than Beren, she was well versed in an existence far removed from his experience, and he eagerly accepted her advice, her friendship, and her tutoring.

She read to him. And Beren listened, rapt, to things beyond his ken, to tales of kings and knights and brave deeds and beautiful ladies. And he had taken them all as gospel. Beren blew out a breath at his own innocence. But Guenivere, with her artless enthusiasm, had made it hard not to believe and take to heart each word she spoke.

She had loved the stories of Arthur and his round table. With her name, who could blame her? But now Beren wondered whether Clement had indulged his daughter's love of fanciful tales too freely.

For the daughter of the castle had filled Beren's head with dreams he never otherwise would have had: to become a knight. And not only must he rise to such an honor, but he must accomplish great deeds and win his lady fair. *Just like Parzival.*

The name brought an ache to Beren's chest, for he well remembered the stories that were Guenivere's favorites: those of Parzival. Despite various spellings and interpretations, they all concerned a boy raised in the woods, ignorant of worldly things. Upon meeting some knights, Parzival decides to take up that life himself.

There were different adventures and versions of the classic, but most dear to Guenivere were the ones where the hero was discovered to be the lost heir to a kingdom, won his quest for the Grail, and married his true love, Condwiramurs. *'Twas A love so deep, so ethereal, that he did not think of making love to her for three nights after their wedding.*

Beren loosed a sigh. The dreams he had back then! And Guenivere fed them, nurturing his hopes, egging him on with tales of glory until his vision of knighthood, so fiercely desired, bore very little resemblance to the harsh reality. 'Twas a difference he soon discovered, for Clement was called to war by his liege and Beren went to serve him. There, on the battlefield, he was girded with a sword and named a knight.

He must have seemed much like Parzival, ignorant and foolish, and lucky he did not live in a land where only those of noble birth could become knights. Although the tales always gave the hero noble lineage, even when unknown, Beren never miraculously found himself to be anything other than what he was. A poor orphan boy of low birth, unworthy, he always reached for those things that were above him, scaling heights that were beyond his grasp... just like these.

Looking up, Beren again saw the cliffs of his childhood, and his heart pounded out a fierce rhythm that once more dispelled despair. This stone had weathered the tests of time, the continuous onslaught of the waves, yet still rose, fierce and proud, into the sky. Feasting his eyes upon the tall faces, he admired each rise like another man would a lover or a friend. And he let himself remember the feel of the climb, both challenge and conquest.

Beren's gaze lit upon his old paths, but he walked on, studying the face of the rock and seeking new routes, where others saw naught except a sheer precipice. He searched, and he planned. Then, when at last he had found the perfect spot, he began his climb.

As he had discovered the other night, his fingers no longer possessed the strength they once had, but his eye was unerring, charting a route among the faint dips and tiny outcroppings. And all during the long, grueling ascent, he concentrated on nothing except the move ahead until at last he reached the summit, weary and triumphant.

Beren gazed down from the same dizzying heights that he had years before, but he found his perspective was different now. Long ago, he had stood here and looked out and seen opportunities in the challenges of the climb, the only ones open to him. Now he saw accomplishments, and not just the striving against rock, but his achievements out in the world that he had once seen only from a distance.

Up here the air seemed more fresh, his mind more clear, as if all the debris of the years had been blown away by the brisk breeze off the water. From this vantage point, just as he could see farther than from anywhere else, Beren could see deeper within himself.

And in that moment of clarity, he realized that whatever his antecedents, he was unlike other men. He had forged a new road for himself, taking the untrodden path, the perilous one that rose straight up into the clouds.

What did it matter if his father were some forgotten king or the meanest villein? Beren had made of himself what he willed. But like a child fearing the specter in the darkness, he had let the question of his parentage control him. If not, he would have returned to claim his bride long ago. But no more would he bow to the past or hide from it, or imagine the judgments of others. For he knew who he was.

Was he not Sir Berenger Brewer, foremost knight and lord of great lands? Beren threw back his head and laughed with a freedom he had never known before.

Guenivere pressed her hands against her pounding temples, though 'twas not the only part of her body that pained her. She ached in private places this morn. And worse yet, her heart, an organ she had long pronounced dead, was stirring once more. She moved her palms downward, over her eyes, where the tears she had thought finished years ago threatened to fall, just as they had last night.

Last night. All too well, Guenivere remembered staring into the fire, wary and uncertain, only to see Beren burst in, like the stuff of dreams, to kneel at her feet. Who could blame her for losing her composure?

But she should not have spoken so freely or confessed to the feelings she had hidden for so long. And most of all, she should not have succumbed, at last, to the temptation of his touch.

If only the night had not been so beautiful. Guenivere's throat constricted, adding to her discomfort. She drew a deep breath, frantically grasping for her usual self-possession. She could not let others see her like this, especially Beren. She had already admitted too much weakness to him, which he had exploited easily enough.

Guenivere sighed, a faint despairing sound. She was being unfair, and she knew it. Beren had not taken advantage of her, for at any time during their night of passion, she could have denied him. But she had not. Instead, she had embraced him, reveling in the fulfillment of all her hopes. *Except one.*

Though he had plied her with sweet words, Beren never said what she had yearned to hear. He had explained his absence glibly enough, but what of his feelings? Although Guenivere racked her mind, the memory of their speech was hazy, overwhelmed by what had followed. And now she found herself belatedly advising caution, an act that resembled throwing water upon the remains of a building that had already burned to the ground.

Guenivere felt her cheeks flame. Burn was right. From the moment he kissed her, she had been lost, a creature of heat and desire. The things he had done to her! Guenivere had never imagined that a man might press his mouth to every part of her. And she did not protest, for it had been Beren who touched her, Beren whose hard body moved over her, Beren who thrust inside her until she cried out in ecstasy.

Guenivere covered her hot cheeks with her palms, moaning

softly as memories washed over her. How could she distance her heart from such intimacies?

And this morning had been no better, for she had awoken in his arms, feeling safe and warm and blissful for one long, precious moment before she had returned to her senses. Then she had fled the naked male beside her, the bed where she had lost her maidenhead, and the room that no longer seemed her own.

But there was no escaping the body that had betrayed her, and Guenivere had roamed restlessly, unwilling to let others see her distress. Finally, she had sought out the quiet of the tiny solar, shooing away any who would disturb her. A trencher of uneaten food lay nearby, but Guenivere ignored it, walking to the narrow window to stare out sightlessly.

Last night she had surrendered to pleasure, but no matter how much her body had enjoyed its initiation, she told herself not to feel anything beyond the throes of passion. For, sooner or later, Beren would be gone again, lost forever to his fine estates and royal companions, while her place was here. And she would once again be naught but a forgotten piece of his past.

Guenivere had lived through that torment once, somehow finding the strength to go on, but she would not risk her heart again. In truth, she didn't think she could endure another breakage of that tender organ. But meanwhile, what was she to do? How was she to distance herself from the man who had invaded her world, her mind, and her bed?

As if her very thoughts had summoned him to mock them, Guenivere heard Beren's unmistakable strides as he walked into the room. Turning slowly to greet him, she drew in a sharp, painful breath.

Whether because of the intimacy they had shared or something else, he appeared different today to her eyes. Taller. Broader. Stronger, yet more gentle. And so handsome that she wanted to weep at the sight of him. She swallowed hard.

"My lady," he said. His low voice reminded her of whispers in the dark, and Guenivere heard herself make a soft, helpless noise. Who knows what might have happened next? Would she have fallen back into his arms or fled the chamber like a frightened hare? Luckily, she did not have to make that choice, for Beren's entrance was soon followed by another as a boy raced into the room like an eager pup.

"My lord, my lord!" he said.

"Yes, Farman, what is it?" Beren asked, giving the boy a smile that made Guenivere's knees so weak she sought a seat. She sank down upon a settle, entwining her hands in her lap to keep them from trembling.

"My lord, a messenger has come from your demesne!"

"Who is it?" Beren asked, his smile fading into a serious expression.

The youth shook his head. "I knew him not. He did not linger, but bade me give you the message and sped away."

Beren's dark brows drew together. "And just what was his message?"

"That you are needed at your lands and must return at once."

Guenivere shuddered as something between a laugh and a sob rose in her throat and was quickly choked back. Even though she had warned herself of Beren's departure all morning, she had never expected it to come so soon. *After one night.* She twisted her fingers in her lap in an effort to maintain her composure.

"Did he say what was the problem?" Beren asked.

Although Guenivere still listened, all her thoughts and will were brought to bear upon maintaining her dignity. She lifted her chin and drew a deep breath.

"No," the youth said. "Only that it was urgent that you return immediately. Perhaps the king is there, waiting for you?"

"I doubt that," Beren said. Guenivere saw him rub a hand over his face and thought she heard him mutter a low curse. "I would prefer to have more information, so that I might judge for myself the necessity of going."

The reason mattered little to Guenivere, who cared only that he had been called away. And gradually, as she regained control of her wildly careening emotions, she told herself that this summons was a good thing. 'Twas better for him to go at once, rather than tarry here, tempting her to give her heart to him again.

After another whispered oath, he sighed. "Very well. Tell the men to prepare to leave," Beren said. He stood watching until the youth disappeared through the doorway, then turned to Guenivere, his face somber. What now? Would he pretend regret?

"As you heard, I am needed at my own demesne," he said, with a rather awkward gesture of his hand.

"Yes, though I find it odd that the man delivering this vital request did not stay long enough to discuss it with you," Guenivere said. Suddenly, she was struck by a dark, painful suspicion. Was there really a message? Or had Beren tired of her so quickly that he must invent an excuse to leave?

"I admit 'tis unusual, but thus did the messenger from Brandeth leave his summons," Beren said. "I can either send a man or go myself, but if 'tis truly a matter of importance I hesitate to wait." He paused to gaze at her directly. "How soon can you be ready to depart?"

Guenivere jerked in surprise. "What?"

"When are you prepared to go?"

"What do you mean?" Guenivere asked, her pulse pounding.

Beren eyed her quizzically. "You are my wife now, so I would have you with me," he said, as though stating the obvious.

"I am not going anywhere!" Guenivere said. "This is my home, and my people need me." She felt panic seize her, constricting her breath, and she struggled to draw in a deep draught of air. She had sought to wed Beren in order to avoid just such a wrench from Brandeth and all that she loved. How could he think that she would willingly leave it now?

Unlike Beren, Guenivere had no wish to see other places or foreign lands, to wander amidst strangers or live among those she knew not. For one terrifying moment, she envisioned a future of being shuttled from castle to court to manor, forgotten by Beren and yet not free to return to her home.

Gripped by fear, she lashed out. "Why would I want to be dragged about like a useless appendage?"

Beren's eyes narrowed. "I thought—" he began, then he paused, as if to consider his words. "Surely, you cannot think yourself useless! I wish for your companionship and advice. And though I have done a lot of traveling, I hope to be able to settle down now that I am married with lands of my own."

"At your demesne," Guenivere said dully. When Beren nodded, she lifted her chin. "That was not part of our bargain."

"Neither was last night!" Beren said. "Yet you cannot deny what happened between us."

Guenivere's insides seemed to roll and pitch with a hot mixture of shame and loss and anger. "Am I to be so grateful for your attentions at this late date that I am willing to be wrested from my home now and forever?"

Beren blinked, as if she had struck him, and his expression hardened into the threatening knight she had first seen upon his return. But Guenivere refused to be intimidated. "Perhaps you have forgotten our conversation upon your arrival," she said, as calmly as she could muster. "But I married you so that I could remain here and hold Brandeth for my own."

If he had looked dangerous before, Beren now appeared positively deadly. His dark brows lowered, his beautiful mouth tightened, and his strong body grew taut. "And that is it? That is the only reason?" he demanded.

"Can you think of another?" Guenivere asked.

For a long moment they stared at each other in silent challenge. Then Beren loosed a harsh breath. "No," he said. And he turned on his heel and stalked out.

Beren's rage had taken him as far as he could lead his men during what remained of the daylight hours, but a night spent alone in a cheerless abbey had tempered his fury and hurt. And now, riding across flat lands with no sight of the sea,

Beren had cause to consider his rash departure.

What had happened? Upon waking from the most glorious night of his life, Beren had sensed that all was not well with his wife. But he had been struggling with his own demons. And instead of talking with her, he had climbed the cliffs. Although he returned euphoric from that foray, after coming to terms with his past, Beren had not stopped to wonder what Guenivere was thinking.

During their night together, she had accused him of betraying her faith. Did he expect one night of passion to heal her wounds and cure her womanly ills?

Beren shook his head at his own folly. The urgency of the summons to return home had caught him off guard and left him few options. But he should have made time for what meant more to him than all else: Guenivere.

Although her words had hurt his pride, that pride was cold comfort now. She had been cool at their parting, but what of the night before when she had melted in his arms, when she had cried for what might have been between them?

Beren swore under his breath. Instead of storming off, he should have questioned her feelings and admitted his own. He should have explained the doubts that had kept him from her all those years. And he should have offered up the love that he felt for her, then, now, and always. It had been the one constant in his life. *Until tested.*

Beren frowned at that truth. Since the first moment he met her, Guenivere had been the force that drove him onward, the greatest height to which he aspired, the dream that he held close. And now that all was within his reach, would he throw it all away? His mouth tightening with determination, Beren held up his hand and called to his men. He had no idea what pressing problems awaited him at his demesne, but they would have to wait.

He had more important things to do.

CHAPTER SIX

Guenivere stood at the window of the solar, looking out into the distance, though she wasn't sure what she sought in the windswept heights. She certainly didn't expect to see Beren. He had been gone already a day and a night and nearly another day, yet Guenivere felt her sense of loss growing, not lessening.

Drawing a deep breath, she searched for the composure that had stood her well these last few years, but she no longer seemed able to muster it. Unwilling to face the people she called her own, Guenivere kept to the solar, disdaining all company. Was it any wonder she felt so sad and alone? But even as she would delude herself, Guenivere knew it was not Alys or any other resident of Brandeth for whom she pined.

She could not understand the return of the old, familiar feeling of missing Beren when this time she had wanted him to be gone about his business, leaving her free to run her father's keep. Yet, somehow her heritage no longer seemed as vital as it once had.

Brandeth still was important to her, but without her father, she had no one here to tend, to cherish. If only she had more family, but there was no one... unless Beren's seed had taken root.

Gingerly, Guenivere touched her stomach, hoping against hope that she might carry his child, and a flush rose in her cheeks as a certain joy dispelled her gloom. But would she raise the babe alone? Although her heart pounded out a denial, what other choice did she have?

And if there was no child?

Suddenly, Guenivere couldn't bear to think of the long, lonely years ahead, so different from what she had planned with cool calculation. She had thought herself independent, needing no man to order her about. She had summoned Beren in a desperate effort to save her lands and the way of life she had known. But now Guenivere wondered if something else hadn't prompted her decision.

Perhaps, in her grief at her father's passing, she had reached out blindly to the only other person she had ever loved. And he had come, reluctantly at first, but determined to take her to wife in good faith. Yet, instead of embracing this new chance for happiness, Guenivere had turned away, unwilling to risk her heart again.

Or so she told herself. Lifting a hand to her mouth, Guenivere made a low sound of anguish as she recognized the truth, at last. Despite all her claims to the contrary, her heart was already engaged. It had been since the first time she had seen the boy named Beren. And not all the years since or their long separation had diminished her feelings.

"Are you well, lady?" The sound of a voice made her turn in startlement, for she had heard no one enter the chamber. For one wild moment, she wondered whether her thoughts had conjured Beren himself. But it was only one of the knights of the keep, eyeing her in question.

Irritated by the intrusion, Guenivere straightened and tried to recover her poise, though she knew her eyes were damp. "What is it, Crispin?" she asked. The old knight had no love for those of ignoble birth who sought to better themselves at his craft, and Guenivere wondered whether he celebrated her husband's departure. At the thought, a tear loosed and slipped down her cheek.

"My lady! You are not well," Crispin said, looking alarmed. "Please sit down, and I will call one of your handmaidens."

Crispin had good cause to be anxious, Guenivere thought, for ever she had hidden her yearning and grief from her people, unknowingly distancing herself from them, as well. Perhaps it was time to rejoin humanity.

"Do not call the ladies to me, for they can do naught for what ails me," she said. " No one can. Have you not heard? My husband has gone away."

Her words seemed to stun the old knight beyond speech,

and Guenivere might have laughed at his stunned expression had her heart been less heavy.

"My lady, I do not understand. I thought this marriage of yours was an alliance of necessity— and beneath you," Crispin said stiffly.

"I forgive you your confusion, for I claimed to act for my people and used whatever means necessary to bring Beren here," Guenivere said. And she felt better for the admission.

Crispin's look of bewilderment gave way to a fierce expression. "He has dazzled you with his new title and power, but those are the things he values. He left you behind swiftly enough to increase them!"

Startled, Guenivere could not understand Crispin's sudden agitation. Nor could she let him continue in his mistaken belief that Beren had abandoned her once more. "But I could have gone with him, as he wished."

"My lady! Your place is here, not off with some upstart urchin who would set you aside for his own advancement."

Guenivere lifted her brows at this open insult to her husband, and more subtly, to herself. "You would make my decisions for me now?"

Crispin appeared uncomfortable yet determined. "I know only that Berenger Brewere is naught but an orphan of lowly birth, a brewer's brat unfit to kiss the hem of your gown!"

"You forget yourself, Sir Knight," Guenivere said coolly. "I will hear no slurs against my husband."

Crispin sent her a dark look, his face grim. "A husband who is gone, never to return, for I have proven his fealty."

At Crispin's words Guenivere went cold. She had sensed something was not right in the knight's manner and speech, but had blamed his old rancor toward Beren. Now, she remembered the strangeness of the summons that Beren received, including her suspicions about the source of the message. And she wondered whether Crispin had been the one to manufacture it.

"And just how did you prove Beren's lack? Did you have

something to do with the urgent call back to his lands?" Guenivere asked.

Crispin's face grew ruddy, but he did not hesitate. "I will not lie to you, lady. I had another feign the message that called him away. But I did it for you, lest you think he has changed, for he has not."

"You seem privy to much of my husband's mind. You know him so well?" Guenivere asked, her tone venomous. Here was a bitter discovery indeed, for she and Beren had enough difficulties, without malicious interference.

"I know him, yes, for what he is, a nameless riffraff who sought always to take the place of his betters!"

"And think you I care for your opinion?" Gueniverc asked.

Crispin flushed, but made no apology. "Who else would save you from yourself? Berate me if you will, but I could not stand to see you debase yourself again for that whoreson, who so easily forgot you and the lord who raised him up! Your father would—"

Guenivere stopped his speech with her own. "My father would have summoned Beren back long ago, had I allowed him. But I let my foolish pride stand in the way of happiness. And now I suffer for the sake of your vanity when I should not."

"But—"

Guenivere cut him off with an imperious wave of her hand. "Bid a train be readied for me, so I might go to my husband and beg forgiveness for my behavior and your own!"

Crispin looked as though he might keel over from apoplexy, but Guenivere had no sympathy for the man who had taken it upon himself to sunder her marriage. If not for the summons, she and Beren might have resolved their differences. Instead, the abruptness of his departure had roused her words against him.

Now, she must try to make amends for that and more. For, if Beren returned to his lands only to find the message was false, he would lay the blame at her feet.

"You cannot mean to leave at this hour." Crispin said. "Perhaps, I acted out of hand, but do not endanger yourself, my lady, I beg you." The old knight seemed sincere, and Guenivere stole a glance out the window where the sun was sinking low, making travel unwise.

"Tomorrow then," she said, although she despised the delay. "But send out a messenger at once to tell Sir Brewere of my coming. Unless you cannot be trusted to do my bidding?" Guenivere asked the question coldly, letting the man see her displeasure. He deserved far worse for his treachery, but she would leave his fate up to Sir Berenger Brewere, Lord of Brandeth.

"By your command, my lady," Crispin said, bowing low, though stiffly.

It was late by the time Beren reached Brandeth. He had to rouse a sleepy guard at the gate, who sent them through with both surprise and welcome. Would that he receive the same, or better, from his lady, Beren thought. But whatever Guenivere's greeting, he was not leaving until all was settled between them, one way or another, and all that needed to be spoken was said.

Assuming that her door was barred for the night, Beren again walked through the bailey to look up at her window. He had no intention of entreating her through a wooden barrier, so once more, he climbed the stone face, familiar now. And by the time he reached the opening, he was flush with the exhilaration of his ascent. Lifting himself up and over, he dropped to the floor inside her chamber.

This time, she was not expecting him, so she was abed. And memories of the night they had spent there fired Beren's blood and firmed his resolve. Without hesitation, he pulled back the curtains, and her name escaped his lips like a prayer.

Although he had time to consider his words during the ride back to Brandeth, the sight of Guenivere gilded by moonlight robbed Beren of his speech. He stood there, silent and staring, as she opened her eyes. And for a long moment, they gazed upon one another. Finally, Beren forced his lips to move, but before he could make a sound, his wife threw herself into his arms.

He drew her close, so startled by this unexpected response that for a moment, he wondered whether he was dreaming, even though she was the one roused from slumber. He choked back a groan, for the warmth of her greeting drove away a chill that had been lying on his heart for years beyond count.

"Beren! How came you here? Did you get my message?" she asked, raising her head to look into his face.

Beren shook his head. "I received no summons, except that of my own desire." He lifted his hands to her shoulders, holding her there as he watched her, willing her to see that he spoke the truth.

"I cannot let you go, not after living my dream—if only for one night," Beren said. "You are all I ever hoped for, all I ever wanted, the sole reason for my striving and for any success I have had. And should you accept me as your husband, now and always, I will stay here with you. I will give up my own lands, if I must, for they are nothing without you. My home is wherever you are."

Guenivere looked as if she might speak, but Beren would have his say. "I have loved you since our very first meeting. But I did not return for fear you would refuse me. The belief that my ignoble blood made me unworthy kept me away."

Beren paused to take a deep breath, his gaze never leaving hers. "For no matter how much you might wish it, I am not Parzival."

Guenivere shook her head. "But I always accepted you as you are. 'Twas you who would not. 'Twas you who valued knighthood and money and lands, not I. Although I admit to a young girls' fascination with the romances, I did not want to marry any of those heroes. Nor did I seek to make you into one. I only wished you to see that you could do anything with your life that you wished. And you did, succeeding beyond imagining!"

Guenivere lifted her hands to cup his face. "As proud as I

was, that success and the new life it brought you seemed to hold no place for me. But I was wrong to let you leave without me. I, too, was afraid—of risking my heart."

She shook her head, her expression bleak. "'Twas not until I let you go that I realized I had never stopped loving you. But then and now, I wanted only you, the real you, the boy I knew and the man he became, not a fanciful hero of song or story."

Beren felt as though the weight of the world had slipped from his shoulders, leaving him no longer bound to the earth, like a man who has climbed the highest heights. He nearly threw back his head and laughed with the pure pleasure of this triumph, greater than all others.

"I am glad to hear you say so, for I am no hero, real or imagined," Beren said. "Although I tried to emulate your ideal, I never found the Grail or a lost father or even a royal uncle."

He took her hands in his. "But I discovered one thing," he said. "All the adventures and achievements of a lifetime are worth little without love. Those long years without you were but half living, and I am thankful to have made my way home at last."

Guenivere kissed him then, a sweet communion that promised far more. "Despite your protestations to the contrary, you would have done Parzival proud," she said. "Indeed, there is only one thing missing from this happy ending."

"What is that?" Beren asked, a bit warily.

"We have no twin sons to awaken and welcome you home," she said, referring once more to her favorite story. But Beren did not mind, for his heart was too full.

"We'll have to work on that," he said, with a grin.

'Twas a vow he would honor this night—and all others.

ABOUT THE AUTHOR

Deborah Simmons began her writing career as a journalist, but left non-fiction for the world of happily ever afters. She's the author of twenty-eight novels and novellas published by Avon, Harlequin, and Berkley, as well as a romantic comedy. Among them are a USA Today Bestselling anthology and her popular series on the medieval de Burgh family.

Her books *A Lady of Distinction* and *The Gentleman Thief* were finalists for Romance Writers of America's annual RITA competition. And two other releases, *The Gentleman's Quest* and *Glory the Rake*, were up for The Daphne du Maurier Award of Excellence for Mystery/Suspense. Her work has been translated and published in more than thirty countries, with graphic novel editions available in Japanese.

DeborahSimmons.com
Facebook.com/authorDeborahSimmons

WORKS BY DEBORAH SIMMONS:

A Heart's Masquerade
Fortune Hunter
Silent Heart
The Squire's Daughter
The Devil's Lady
The Vicar's Daughter
Taming the Wolf
The Devil Earl
Maiden Bride
Tempting Kate
A Wish for Noel
The de Burgh Bride
The Last Rogue
Robber Bride
The Unexpected Guest
The Gentleman Thief
My Lord de Burgh
The Companion
The Bachelor Knight
My Lady de Burgh
The Notorious Duke
A Man of Many Talents
A Lady of Distinction
The Dark Viscount
Reynold de Burgh: The Dark Knight
The Gentleman's Quest
Glory and the Rake
The Last de Burgh
It Had to Be You

www.ingramcontent.com/pod-product-compliance
Lightning Source LLC
Chambersburg PA
CBHW071223170626
46809CB00005BA/1917